This Book Belongs to:

Mickey's Young Readers Library

VOLUME
11

Huey, Dewey, and Louie Meet the Witch

STORY BY JUSTINE KORMAN

Activities by Thoburn Educational Enterprises, Inc.

A BANTAM BOOK

NEW YORK · TORONTO · LONDON · SYDNEY · AUCKLAND

One day, Huey, Dewey, and Louie went off to find adventure in a nearby forest.

"We're down to our last piece of bread, our last little carrot, and one bare soup bone," Dewey told his brothers.

"This doesn't seem like much of an adventure," Huey complained.

"It could be worse," Louie sighed. "We could be lost."

"Do you know where we are?" Huey asked him.

Louie looked around the dark woods. He had no idea where they were.

"At least it isn't raining," Dewey said.

But just then, they heard thunder.

"That's great," Louie moaned. "We're hungry. It's getting dark. And now there's a storm on the way."

The wind began to blow wildly through the trees. The boys couldn't decide what to do first—find a place to sleep, or find something to eat.

"Let's rest while we decide what to do," Huey said. Then he looked up at the sound of a tiny chirp. There he saw a skinny little bird that began to sing a lovely song. When the song was over, the hungry bird looked at the bread in Huey's hand.

"You poor thing. You must be starving," Huey said. Then he gave the bird the bread.

"What have you done?" cried Dewey and Louie. "That was our last piece of bread."

"Do unto others as you would have others do unto you," said Huey. "If I were a hungry bird alone in the forest, I would want someone to give me some bread," he added.

"Thank you, young sir. I will not forget your kindness," the bird chirped.

"You-you-you can talk?" Huey asked. Dewey
and Louie were too surprised to ask anything at all.

"Yes," the bird answered. "You see, I am under
a witch's spell—the witch who lives in the cottage at
the end of this path. Whatever you do, don't go
there—or she'll put a spell on you!"

And with this warning, the bird flew away.

"I'm not afraid of any old witch," Huey said.

"After all, we're looking for adventure, aren't we? Let's go see this witch for ourselves," added Louie. "What do you think, Dewey?" he asked.

But Dewey wasn't listening. He was looking at a horse standing nearby.

"I'm going to catch that horse and take a ride," Dewey called to his brothers.

When Dewey saw how thin and tired the horse looked, he changed his mind.

"Poor thing," he whispered. "I've got something for you." Then he reached into his pocket and gave the horse his very last carrot—before Huey and Louie could stop him.

"That's just great!" complained Louie. "No bread, no carrot—all we have left is one bare soup bone."

"Well, I'm sorry, but if I were a hungry horse, I'd want someone to feed me."

"I will not forget your kindness," the horse told Dewey.

"Why—you must be under a witch's spell, too, just like the bird we met before!" Huey exclaimed.

The horse nodded. "Run from the witch," he warned. Then he galloped away.

Just then, a dog came running out of the forest.

"Well, hello there!" Louie said. Without a second thought, Louie gave the dog the soup bone. Huey and Dewey smiled.

"I will not forget your kindness," the dog told Louie. Then it, too, ran off, warning, "Run away from the witch while you still can!"

The three boys looked at each other. Now they had nothing to eat *and* no place to sleep. All of a sudden, they sniffed a delicious smell.

"It's coming from over there!" pointed Huey. He
was pointing to the witch's cottage.

The growling of their stomachs made them
forget the animals' warnings. They followed the
delicious smell right up to the cottage. The cottage
looked warm and cozy—and there was a wonderful
smell of soup!

The boys knocked on the wooden door.
"What do you want?" a voice asked.
"Food and a place to sleep," Louie replied.
The old witch opened the door and looked at the boys.
"All right," she said. "I'll give you soup and a bed if you'll each give me one day's work."
"It's a deal," the boys agreed, as they went in.

At once the boys sat at the table and started to eat. The soup tasted even better than it smelled. And when their happy stomachs were full, the witch gave them each a blanket and a place by the fire. Soon the three adventurers were fast asleep.

The next morning, the witch told the boys what to do.

"You fill this basket with apples from the top of those three giant apple trees," she told Huey. Then she handed him a huge apple basket.

"You dig a hole big enough to swim in," she told Louie. Then she handed him a small spoon.

"And you use this cup to fill the swimming hole with water from the lake," she told Dewey.

"We can't do these jobs!" cried the boys.

The witch laughed a wicked laugh. "I forgot to tell you one thing. If you don't finish your jobs by dark, I'll turn you all into sheep. I need some wool to make some nice warm pairs of socks!" Then she went inside to take a nap.

"What are we going to do?" Louie asked his brothers.

"Baa, baa, baa," Huey sang. "We might as well get used to it," he said. "There's no way we can do what she asks."

Suddenly an apple fell into the huge apple basket. Huey looked up. There he saw the bird to which he had given the piece of bread.

"I didn't forget. You helped me," the bird chirped to Huey. "Now, I'll help you." And the bird began to pick the apples from the giant apple trees until Huey's basket was full.

"And you helped us," said the horse and the dog. "Now we'll help you, too." Then the dog began to dig a hole deep enough for the witch to swim in. Next, the horse took Dewey on its back and galloped back and forth from the lake, carrying cups full of water.

Before dark every job was done.

"You have been very kind," the boys told their animal friends. "Is there some other way we can be of help to you?" the boys asked.

"Take the witch's wand before she wakes up. Next, run to the edge of the forest and break the wand in two. That will end her wicked spells and take away her powers. Then we will meet you there as soon as we can."

Huey, Dewey, and Louie tiptoed into the cottage where the witch was fast asleep. They slipped the magic wand out of her pocket and ran as fast as they could to the edge of the forest.

When the witch woke up and went outside, she couldn't believe her eyes. All her jobs had been done.

"Those horrible boys! I'll turn them into sheep anyway," she decided. She reached into her pocket for her magic wand.

"It's gone!" she cried. "I'll get those boys for this!" she shouted.

The witch began to run through the woods. There she came upon the little bird.

"Lead me to those three terrible boys!" the witch cried out.

"I won't," the tiny bird replied. "They were kind to me and you were not." And with that off flew the bird.

The witch ran along the path in the forest, hoping to catch sight of the boys. Just then she spotted the dog.

"Help me find those boys," the witch shouted.

"I won't," the dog barked. "They were kind to me and you were not." Then he ran in circles around the witch, making her quite dizzy before he ran off into the woods.

The witch crashed angrily through the woods. When she came to the horse, she jumped on and shouted, "Carry me to those boys!"

"I won't," the horse neighed.

"Let me guess," the witch said. "They were kind to you and I was not."

"That's right," nodded the horse. And he would not budge.

"Never mind!" she cried. "I'll find them myself.
You can't get good enchanted animals these days."
She ran back to her house and pulled out her
broomstick. Then she flew through the forest, looking
for Huey, Dewey, Louie, and her magic wand!

The witch got to the edge of the forest just in
time to see Louie break her wand in two.

As the wand snapped, the broomstick dropped to the ground. The unhappy witch fell to the ground with it. All of her magic spells were broken at last!

In the very minute that the witch lost her magic, the bird, the dog, and the horse turned back into three men.

The shortest one explained to Huey, Dewey, and Louie, "We were adventurers, too. The witch tricked us the same way she tricked you."

"But we had no one to help us at all!" added the tallest one.

After thanking Huey, Dewey, and Louie once again for their kindness, the three young men went off to continue their adventures. They told the boys they would be sure to watch out for witches from now on!

The boys waved a cheery good-bye to them.

Just then the witch spoke up.

"That's all fine and good for you adventurers," she scolded. "But now that you've broken my magic wand, how will I get things done?"

"Do you mean that you can't make that delicious magic soup anymore?" Huey asked.

"Oh that soup isn't magic," explained the witch. "My grandmother taught me how to make it."

That gave Dewey an idea. He whispered the plan to his brothers.

"If I were a witch without a wand alone in the forest ..." Huey began.

"... you'd want someone to help you out!" Dewey and Louie finished.

So the boys hammered and sawed, painted and cleaned until the witch's cottage looked all new.

When they were done, the witch's cottage was turned into a cozy little restaurant. All through the forest, the boys put up signs that said, "Grand Opening—Good Witch Restaurant. Just follow your nose. Try our magical soup!"

Once people tasted the delicious soup, they came from far and wide to eat at the Good Witch Restaurant.

And the witch was the happiest person of all—
for she had learned something very important. She
could make friends—like magic—just by being as
nice to others as she wanted them to be to her.

And the good witch told Huey, Dewey, and
Louie, "Whenever you grow tired or hungry on your
adventures, you will always find free soup and a
place to rest at the Good Witch Restaurant."

Helping Hands

Match each boy to the animal he helped in the story. Do you remember in which order the boys met the animals?

After your child does the activities in this book, refer to the *Young Readers Guide* for the answers to these activities and for additional games, activities, and ideas.

The Witch's Tale

The witch in this book wants you to think about "her" side of the story.

1. Why do you think the witch invited Huey, Dewey, and Louie into her house for dinner?

2. How did the witch feel when she found out that Huey, Dewey, and Louie had taken her wand? What did she do about it?

3. How did the witch feel when she no longer had her magic powers?

4. How do you think she felt when Huey, Dewey, and Louie helped her set up her restaurant?

5. What did the witch learn at the end of the story?

Fun With Words

A Witch-y Message

There's a special message written on the witch's caldron. It's the lesson she learned by the end of the story. Can you figure out what it is? (Hint: Hold this page up to a mirror to help you.)

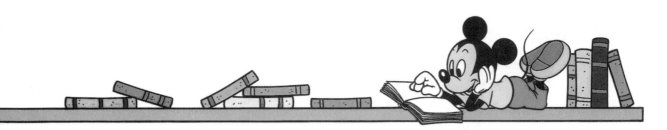

A Witch's Brew

As a special favor to her other witch friends, the Good Witch is trying out a new recipe for witch's brew. To find out what goes into this brew, point to the words *below* the caldron that begin with the same letters as the words that are *above* the caldron.

wand
bird
horse
cottage
dog

webs   beetles   hornet   dragonfly   caterpillar
salt   onions   pepper   tomatoes   meat